This scary-cool
book belongs to

Bailey
....

This edition published by Parragon Books Ltd in 2013 and distributed by

Parragon Inc.
440 Park Avenue South, 13th Floor
New York, NY 10016
www.parragon.com

ISBN 978-1-4723-2743-7

Printed in China

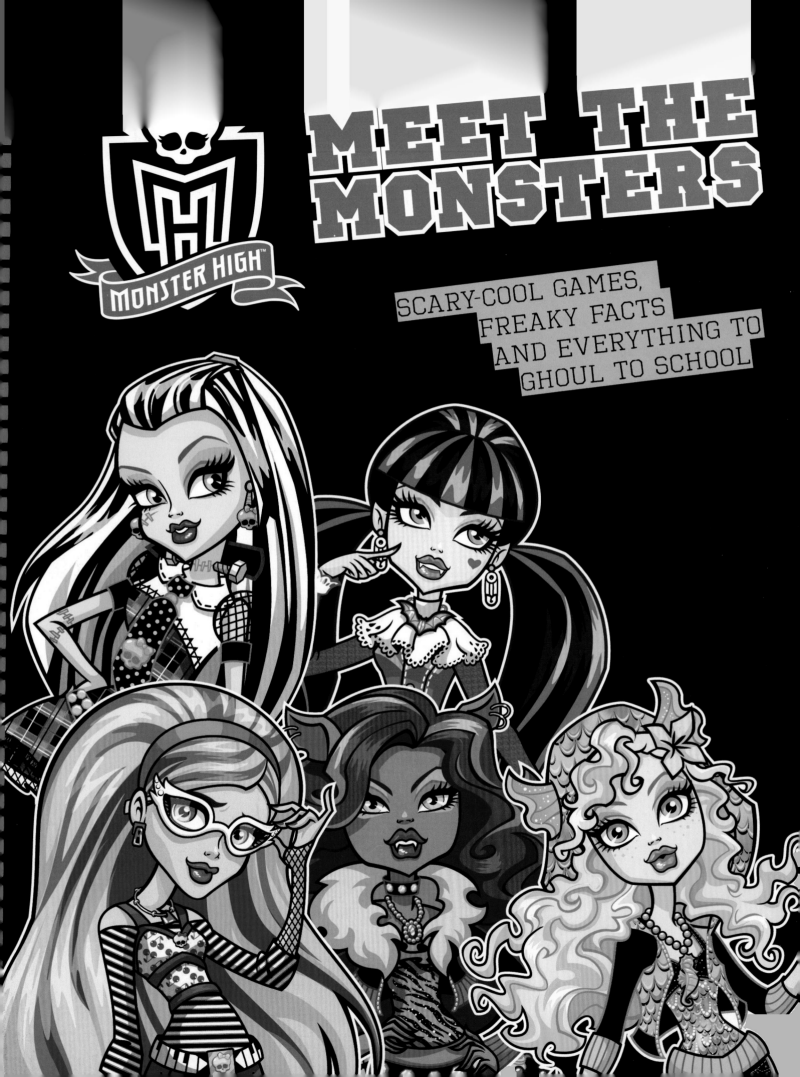

MEET THE MONSTERS

MONSTER HIGH

SCARY-COOL GAMES, FREAKY FACTS AND EVERYTHING TO GHOUL TO SCHOOL

Contents

Welcome to Monster High,

Congratulations on your choice of school. I am certain you will feel at home among our freakily friendly and scarily enthusiastic students. We are very proud of our "fangtastic" test scores—be assured that the deaducation you will receive here is second to none.

The building boasts outstanding facilities, from the state of the art infearmation technology lab to our refurbished casketball courts. We offer an amazing array of extra-scare-icular activities, too.

Work hard, play fair and keep out of trouble. As I always say, "losing your head is no excuse for not doing the right thing".

Headless Headmistress Bloodgood

Sleepy Hollow State B.S., Equestrian Studies
Marie Antoinette AEM M.A., Horticulture/Para-Psychology

SCHOOL RULES:
Respect your fellow monsters
No growling or biting in the halls
iCoffins must be switched off during lessons
Pets are not permitted in the creepateria or classrooms

Exsisto vestri. Exsisto unique. Exsisto a Monasteriense

Frankie Stein

She's the ghoul with the most stylish stitches in school. Made 15 days ago by her dad, Dr. Frankenstein, Frankie is seeing Monster High through new eyes. From chowing down in the creepateria to advanced math with Mr. Mummy, Frankie's totally psyched to be here! Check out her student ID card below and then use the facing page to create your own.

MONSTER HIGH

STUDENT ID CARD

STUDENT: Frankie Stein

AGE: 15 (days)

FAVORITE COLOR: Black and white stripes

PET: Watzit™, the puppy my father Victor put together for me

BEST SUBJECT: History—I'm only 15 days old so it's great to understand where my friends are coming from

WORST SUBJECT: Swimming—I short-circuit when I get wet!

ADDITIONAL INFO: My BFFs are Draculaura and Clawdeen Wolf

My School Die-ary

Ouch! School is so intense right now. I've only been around a couple of weeks so I'm still finding my way around. I just hope that I don't fall apart at the seams with the Scary Aptitude Test looming. Last week my hand flew off in a biteology exam and nearly scalped Deuce Gorgon™! Voltagious fail! There are some scary cute guys at school, but at the moment I just wanna spend time with Ula D™ and Clawdeen. They are ughhsome! Can't wait to invite them over to hang out in my basement lab. I call it 'the fab'. Why?

Because it is!

This is me

STUDENT ID CARD

STUDENT: Bailey Brownce

AGE: 8 years old

FAVORITE COLOR: Pink and PuRPLe

PET: I love animals and dogs

BEST SUBJECT: Math-becaWse numberbonds are soo easy

WORST SUBJECT: I can't anser because I'mg good at it

ADDITIONAL INFO: Pets; I have a bird named birdy a dog Named Pluto and DaiSy!

Ghouls just wanna have fun!

I'm with the BAND

MONSTER HIGH DRAMA FREAK

Draculaura ™

She's the sweetest ghoul at Monster High! Draculaura, or Ula D as she likes to be known, is the gregarious ghoul who is universally liked by her fellow students. Always on the prowl for love, Ula D can't wait to get to the study howl to check out all the ughsome boys. Who knows? Clawd Wolf™ might be there! Draculaura is in such a hurry today, she's dropped her student ID card. Get to know the monster, then help Ula D achieve her killer look.

MONSTER HIGH

STUDENT ID CARD

STUDENT:	Draculaura™
AGE:	1,599 (nearly my sweet 1600th!)
FAVORITE COLOR:	Pink
PET:	Count Fabulous™, my BFF (Bat Friend Forever)
BEST SUBJECT:	Creative Writing—it gives me a chance to write tales about my gorgeous ghoulfriends
WORST SUBJECT:	Geography—after 1,599 years I've been everywhere ... twice!
ADDITIONAL INFO:	I'm a vegetarian. No blood for me, just fruit, veg and iron supplements

Like all vampires, Draculaura can't see her reflection in the mirror, but she still wants to look drop dead gorgeous! Can you help her apply her make-up? Ula D loves pale skin and bitingly slick pink lipgloss. Don't forget her trademark—a cute, heart-shaped beauty spot!

Today is going to be fangtastic!

My School Die-ary

Aaaargh! I've just been to the creepateria to grab a bite and yet again there were no vegetarian options. Guess I'm going to have to start bringing my lunch in, unless I can persuade Headmistress Bloodgood to change the menus. Clawd smiled at me from the next table. Thought I'd died all over again! He's even more ughsome than the Jaundice Brothers.

11

Clawdeen Wolf™

Is there a fiercer fashionista in the whole of Monster High than Clawdeen? That ghoul just oozes confidence. She works hard to look this amazing and when she's done with her beauty regime, it's on to her wicked wardrobe. Never short of furrociously fabulous—and an amazing athlete to boot—Clawdeen makes you want to howl at the Moon!

MONSTER HIGH™

STUDENT ID CARD

STUDENT: Clawdeen Wolf

AGE: 15

FAVORITE COLOR: Gold

PET: Crescent™ the cat

BEST SUBJECT: Economics—I'm gonna need a sharp business brain if I'm going to set up my own fashion empire

WORST SUBJECT: Gym—I can't bear taking off my sky-high heels, but I can still beat Heath Burns™ in track

ADDITIONAL INFO: My fave food is steak, as long as it's rare!

My School Die-ary

It's Fashion Entrepreneurs Club tonight, yay! We're all working hard to design a collection for the 1,313th Fierce Fashion Show. It's gonna be spooktacular! I've asked Frankie to model for me. She tries to be modest, but she's got a freakily perfect figure for fashion—anything looks hot on her. Can't wait to see her strutting her stuff in my new designs!

Fierce Family Foto

Clawdeen comes from a big wolf pack. She has a lot of brothers and one little sister, Howleen. Her older brother is Clawd Wolf. Although they fight like cats and dogs—or cats and wolves—the gang are fiercely loyal, always there for each other no matter what. Clawdeen's lair is filled with photos like this one of her with Clawd and Howleen. Who's who in your pack? Have you got a clutch of brothers, sisters or cousins? Draw you and your peeps in here.

Lagoona Blue ™

Just follow the wet footprints through the school howlways and you'll soon track down Lagoona. Daughter of the Sea Monster, she's a free spirit who's crazy about all things aquatic. No wonder she's the star of Monster High's swimming and surf teams! Lagoona would rather be in the deep blue than the study howl. Sneak a peek at her ID, then doodle along with the water babe.

MONSTER HIGH ™

STUDENT ID CARD

STUDENT: Lagoona Blue

AGE: 15

FAVORITE COLOR: Ocean blue

PET: Neptuna™ the piranha. Don't mind the teeth, she's a total cutie!

BEST SUBJECT: Oceanography—if I can't be in the water, I want to be studying it

WORST SUBJECT: Geology—stones and rubble definitely don't rock my world. Why stick my head in a dry old textbook when I could be creeping out in the Monster High pool?

ADDITIONAL INFO: I'm an exchange student, all the way from the ocean Down Under

My School Die-ary

I can't believe I got dead-tention for sneaking Neptuna into class! Most of the teachers never guess that my purse, which is designed to look like a fishbowl, actually is a fishbowl! My pet piranha wouldn't travel any other way! Now that I've been busted, Mr. Mummy says I've got to write 100 flat-lines.

GHOULS RULE!

Doodles To Die For

Lagoona is a dreadfully dedicated doodler—especially when she's stuck in class! She began these latest designs during a deadly boring clawculus review session. Are you a doodle beast? Fill the remaining space below with your own creeperific creations.

$E=mc^2$

Cleo De Nile ™

Everyone knows Cleo. With her gilt-edged looks and skin-tight bandaged style, she's kind of hard to miss! Miss De Nile is captain of the Monster High fearleading squad and the self-professed queen of the popular crowd in school. Read the Egyptian princess' stellar student ID then pick up some hot tips from her *Teen Scream* magazine article about being the perfect ghoulfriend.

MONSTER HIGH ™

STUDENT ID CARD

STUDENT:	CLEO DE NILE
AGE:	5,842 YEARS (GIVE OR TAKE A YEAR)
FAVORITE COLOR:	GOLD
PET:	HISSETTE™, THE SWEETEST EGYPTIAN COBRA YOU COULD EVER MEET!
BEST SUBJECT:	GEOMETRY—I'VE GOT A NATURAL FLAIR FOR ANY SUBJECT THAT USES TRIANGLES AND PYRAMIDS!
WORST SUBJECT:	HISTORY—BEEN THERE, SEEN THAT, GOT AUTOGRAPHS FROM ANYONE THAT MATTERED
ADDITIONAL INFO:	I MUST BE ALLOWED TO LEAVE SCHOOL BEFORE THE SUN GOES DOWN. I'VE GOT A FREAKY PHOBIA ABOUT IT!

Ghoulfriend Of His Dreams
Cleo's been working on ideas for an article for *Teen Scream* magazine.
She thinks readers will love her top dating tips. Check out her fangtastic plan!

The Ghoulfriend Rules

By Cleo De Nile

1

IMPRESS THE MONSTER OF YOUR DREAMS BY SHOWING OFF YOUR NATURAL TALENTS.
MY FEARLEADING SKILLS HAVE A DAZZLING EFFECT!

2

ALWAYS LOOK PERFECT.

3

MAKE SURE THE MONSTER KNOWS HOW LUCKY HE IS—YOUR TIME IS PRECIOUS!

4

DO NOT INTRODUCE YOUR GHOULFRIEND TO YOUR EVIL ELDER SISTERS. EVER.

5

MAKE THE MOST OF FAMILY HEIRLOOMS—USE THEM TO REPEL RIVALS.
CURSED IDOLS AND FANGED PETS ARE PERFECT!

Can you add some more relationship rules for Cleo and her ghoulfriends?

Loke hise a hd prf/t to school and were golld to school. Love CLEo

MY SCHOOL DIE-ARY

O.M.G! WE ARE GOING TO ACE THE MONSTER MASHIONALS THIS YEAR, BUT NEW GHOUL FRANKIE HAS DEFINITELY ADDED SOMETHING TO THE FEARLEADING TEAM—ALTHOUGH OF COURSE ALL EYES WILL STILL BE ON ME AS THE STAR OF THE SQUAD! DEUCE CAME TO WATCH US AT PRACTICE TODAY. HE'S TAKING ME TO SEE JUSTIN BITER IN CONCERT THIS WEEKEND. GOLDEN!

I don't like the dark—it hides my beauty!

Ghoulia Yelps ™

OK, so she's not the most communicative of students, but then show us a zombie who is! Beneath those horn-rimmed glasses is a smart brain with an awesome appetite for learning. Ghoulia is a loyal friend to Cleo and is by far the smartest monster in school. Check her deets below and then see if you can ace her history homework—the answers are on page 68.

MONSTER HIGH™

STUDENT ID CARD

STUDENT: Ghoulia Yelps

AGE: 16

FAVORITE COLOR: Red

PET: Sir Hoots A Lot™

BEST SUBJECT: Unfortunately the narrow constraints of this question mean I cannot answer. (In other words, I love 'em all!)

WORST SUBJECT: There is something to be learned from every class

ADDITIONAL INFO: Give me a break if I bump into you in the howl—I do not move fast and can't process last minute schedule changes well

1.

Fill in the blanks below to complete an alternative name for the Abominable Snowman.

YETI

2.

Ancient vampire Dracula is said to come from...
a. Argentina ☐
b. The United States ☐
c. Transylvania ☑

3.

In Ancient Egypt, rulers were often buried in tombs within which triangular structures?

.... PYRAMIDS ....

4.

Which metal is most dangerous to a werewolf?
a. Silver ☑
b. Gold ☐
c. Platinum ☐

5.

In Greek mythology, the Goddess Athena punished Medusa by turning her to stone.
True ☐
False ☑

6.

A distant cousin to the Sea Monster, the Loch Ness Monster lurks in which European country?

.... Scoutland ....

YOU CAN'T HURRY GENIUS!

My School Die-ary

Library 2pm

Biteology 3pm

Study Howl 4pm

Fearleading practice 6pm (gotta be on hand to wipe Cleo's brow)

I'm in the middle of a zombie love triangle. Two zombies squared off over me last week outside the creepateria—last time I looked they were still there. Zombie fights are slow!

Spectra Vondergeist™

Pssst! Who's that haunting beauty floating down the corridor? It's only Spectra, the most glamorous ghost at Monster High. If you want to know all the comings and groanings behind the screams in school, then Spectra has to be your ghoul! It's worth doing a quick fact check, however, before you pass on her gossipy gems—the spooky student does have a tendency to embellish.

MONSTER HIGH

STUDENT ID CARD

STUDENT:	Spectra Vondergeist
AGE:	16
FAVORITE COLOR:	Violet
PET:	Rhuen™, my ghost ferret
BEST SUBJECT:	Journalism
WORST SUBJECT:	Math—it's so rigid and un-open to interpretation
ADDITIONAL INFO:	If after a chat with me you suddenly find your school bag is missing, it's probably down to Rhuen™. The word ferret comes from the Latin furittus, meaning 'little thief'. Oops!

Ghouls Rule!

My School Die-ary

OMG, or should I say Oh My Ghoul! I just heard that Nefera de Nile has been drafted in to help the Monster High fearleading squad make the Monster Mashionals. A certain someone (name beginning with C, ending with an O with the letters L and E in it) is spitting more venom than her pet snake. Can't wait to see how that turns out. Hold the front page!

Spectra's Slimetable

Bolts! Frankie accidentally short-circuited the printer when Spectra was printing out her slimetable—now it's all messed up. Can you help Spectra sort out her schedule? Unscramble the anagrams to figure out the subjects she'll be studying, then write the classes into the ghoul's planner. Next check the faculty list and jot each teacher's name underneath.

	LESSON 1	LESSON 2	LESSON 3	LUNCH	LESSON 4
MONDAY	MIKE HOC	LOGOYEBIT	GAGA UNLEADEDS		CLASHYIP CANDIEDAUTO
TUESDAY	GAGA UNLEADEDS	MADRA	ACULLCUWS		EG-GROE-GYP
WEDNESDAY	GRANTEDROOMY	GRANTEDROOMY	LOGOYEBIT		STUDY HOWL
THURSDAY	MADRA	FREE PERIOD	ACULLCUWS		GAGA UNLEADEDS
FRIDAY	CLASHYIP CANDIEDAUTO	GAGA UNLEADEDS	STUDY HOWL		ZIFZ-SKIC

Monster High Faculty

Mr. Where: Drama
Coach Igor: Physical Deaducation
Mr. Hackington: Mad Science
(Biteology, Fizz-icks)
Mr. Lou Zarr: Ge-ogre-phy

Ms. Kindergrubber: Home Ick
Mr. Mummy: Math
(Clawculus, Dragonometry)
Mr. Rotter: Dead Languages

Abbey Bominable™

Abbey had a chilly first week at Monster High. She got involved in a snowball fight with Frankie Stein in class and was sent to see Headmistress Bloodgood. The result? The pair were chained together all day to learn a lesson in bonding! Now that's all behind her, Abbey has settled in well. She and Frankie are firm, frosty friends and everyone's used to Abbey's cool, cold ways.

MONSTER HIGH

STUDENT ID CARD

STUDENT: Abbey Bominable

AGE: 16

FAVORITE COLOR: Ice blue

PET: Shiver, my woolly mammoth

BEST SUBJECT: Math—numbers are the mountain beneath the snow

WORST SUBJECT: Drama

ADDITIONAL INFO: Note to staff: I must be allowed to wear my ice crystal necklace. It perpetuates the coldness of my homeland

Icy Putdowns

Monsters hailing from the icy Himalayas are notoriously short and to the point! Abbey can seem super-harsh sometimes, especially as English is not her first language. Can you match each of her unintentionally cutting comments with the monster on the receiving end?

Cold is the new hot!

Your eyebrows, they are like mountains.

People around here talk too much about too little, sometimes is better to just close the mouth.

This outfit, I think you try much too hard.

You are short—like baby yak.

My School Die-ary

In my country the air is very thin—we cannot be wasting the breath on small talk, so the monsters in school they think I am rude. I am wishing to make the thoughts in my heart and the words from my mouth the same and for the friend who will be patient until that is happening. I think Frankie is already a nice friend to me and Lagoona is much helpful too. These ghouls begin to understand that although I am cold to the touching, I am warm in my heart and have the feelings too.

Operetta ™

Operetta is a cool country diva with a passion for music and a fierce take on rockabilly style. Her immortal musical talents on keyboards (she was home-taught by her dad, the Phantom of the Opera) are matched by her voice, which is literally to die for. Hearing Operetta sing can make the listener lose his or her mind! The monster takes care never to sing live, always recording her melodies.

MONSTER HIGH

STUDENT ID CARD

STUDENT: Operetta

AGE: 16 ... in phantom years

FAVORITE COLOR: Vintage velvet red

PET: Memphis 'Daddy O' Longlegs™, my beloved spider

BEST SUBJECT: Music history—you can't know where you're going if you don't know where you've been

WORST SUBJECT: Mad science

ADDITIONAL INFO: Don't step on my clef-heeled shoes or squish my quiff-haired spider!

My School Die-ary

Grrrness, ughness, great balls of fire! What a day. Had mad science with Mr. Hackington and spent the whole lesson thinking up lyrics for a new song. That crazy chicky Cleo asked me to write one for her guy, Deuce. He is one ughsome monster and she's a lucky lady, so I said I'd help out.

Last term I helped him write a love song for her so I guess this is her reply. Deuce thought my tune was fang-tastic. Cleo told me "if I ever said thank you, I'd say it now".

SHOW YOUR GHOUL SPIRIT

Use this space to pen a song for Operetta to record and play at the 1313th celebrations. Make sure it's suitably spooky in tone—this monster wants to totally rock the party!

25

Comic Book Club

Besides homework, did you know that Ghoulia Yelps has another passion in life? Yup, the zombie can't get enough of comics. Her favorite stories feature anti-hero Dead Fast, but she'll read anything gory and graphic. She even runs Monster High's comic club! The Comic Clubbers have been busy transforming the in-school goings-on into comic strips. Take a freak-peek at Ghoulia's work so far....

Unlife To Live

Ghoulia Yelps was studying on the school steps when....

Ghoulia, we're going for smoothies in free period, want to join us?

O.M.Ra! You're not too busy, you're just sitting there like you do every day!

Nurrgh!

Suddenly a brain-shaped distress signal lit up the sky. Ghoulia sprang into action....

Ghoulia whisked the Headmistress to the salon and back....

Ghoulia! I need to get my hair done for the Superintendent's party tonight, but I'm swamped with paperwork ....

Thanks Ghoulia. I look fabulous!

Next, there was an icy issue at the pool....

Is yours now.

Brrrr, it's ffffreezing!

Monster Match

Psychology—the science of the monster mind—is one of the most fang-scinating subjects on the Monster High scare-iculum. As mad science teacher Mr. Hackington always says, "A dull mind cannot cut the cheese of knowledge." Use Mr. Hackington's flowchart to find out which monster personality you possess. Just answer the questions and follow the arrows!

My ghoulfriends and I love to trawl the maul for clothes

Me and my ghoulfriends love hanging out in my basement

FALSE

FALSE

FALSE

TRUE

My classmates think I'm a voltagious freak

Start

TRUE

TRUE

FALSE

I'm the most laid-back ghoul in school

A dog is every ghoul's best friend

FALSE

Meoww.... Cats are creeperific!

The best thing about school is having fun ... school is fierce!

TRUE

FALSE

FALSE

TRUE

FALSE

You can't beat a makeover creepover with the ghouls

TRUE

I like my pets with fangs

TRUE

FALSE

My classmates think I'm furrociously fabulous

I'm at my most spooktacular in black

My classmates think I'm a freaky sweetie

FALSE

TRUE

FALSE

TRUE

FALSE

FALSE

The best thing about school is the ughsome guys in the corridors

TRUE

Draculaura

You're as friendly and frightfully cheerful as Ula D! Freaky fabulous!

Frankie Stein

Like Frankie you're a high-voltage ghoul, who's enthusiastic and fun.

The best thing about school is phys dead. I'm the fastest ghoul in school

TRUE

TRUE

FALSE

TRUE

I look scarily cute in pink

FALSE

Gold is my color

Clawdeen Wolf

You and Clawdeen are fierce fashionistas, who can hold their own in a crowd.

Cleo and Deuce's Dead-Secret Code

Monster High is big on Dead Languages—the study of ancient tongues. Sadly, Mr. Rotter's lessons are monstrously dull! He won't tolerate pranks and is always asking the principal to expel students. To liven things up, Cleo and Deuce have designed their own secret way of communicating. They've developed a monster mash-up of ancient Greek and Egyptian hieroglyphics!

Use the key at the bottom of the page to figure out the contents of their horror-spondence. Once you've cracked the code, try using it yourself!

Hi Deuce,

I've told Ghoulia we'll take her to the coffin bean after school today and that you're paying. oh and By the way, I'm throwing a party on Saturday Night. Be there and look fangtastic!

Cleo

hey cleo,

DO I really have to pay ...
again? you know I love
To treat you, But I'm
Trying to save up. And
before you totally like,
Lose your bandages, it's
for a surprise for you.
i'll give it to you at
your party.

DEUCE

Code

A B C D E F G H I J K L M N

O P Q R S T U V W X Y Z

Grim Grid

Mr. Rotter, the dead languages teacher, loves grim grids—the monster form of the crossword. He's always asking students to complete them! Try your hand at this one. Make sure you finish before he lumbers around to check on your progress....

Clues

Across

1. Last name of Monster High drama teacher. (5)
2. Pointed teeth seen on vampires and werewolves. (5)
3. _____ of the Opera, father of Operetta. (7)
4. Headmistress Bloodgood's pet. (9)
5. Carnivorous fish often found in the Monster High swimming pool. (7)
6. Physical _____. An active lesson on the Monster High slimetable. (11)
7. Box used for burial and as a locker at Monster High. (6)
8. Last name of the school's home-ick teacher. (13)
9. Metallic color and phrase Cleo uses to describe something awesome. (6)
10. Hard material that victims of Deuce Gorgon's stare find themselves transformed into. (5)
11. Name of a popular monster magazine. (4,6)
12. "It's _____!" Exclamation Frankie's father shouts each morning when seeing his daughter. (5)
13. Clawdeen's favorite food. (5)

Down

1. Name of Frankie's pet. (6)
2. Type of monster; parent of Abbey Bominable. (4)
3. Checked pattern often used on cloth and frequently worn by Frankie. (5)
4. Bright color favored by Draculaura. (4)
5. First name of Miss Vondergeist, a ghostly student at Monster High. (7)
6. Cloth wrappings used in ancient Egypt on bodies and often seen trailing from Cleo de Nile. (8)
7. Monster High activity involving dancing in a group and performing cheers. (11)
8. Monster High version of "Homecoming". (11)
9. Cleo's older sister. (6)
10. Place where Monster High students eat lunch. (11)
11. Skin hydrating product used in large amounts by Lagoona Blue. (11)
12. Word meaning "girlfriend" in the monster world. (11)
13. Team sport like basketball played at Monster High. (10)
14. Species of animal owned as a pet by Jackson Jekyll™ and Holt Hyde™. (9)
15. Website where monsters post video clips. (10)
16. Warm material often worn by Abbey Bominable. (3)
17. Name of Cleo's scaly pet. (8)
18. "The _____". Advice column in teen monster magazine. (6)
19. Slow, uncommunicative type of monster found at Monster High. (6)
20. Cleo is afraid of this.... (4)

Who's Your Monster High Love Match?

There are some spooktacularly hot guys at Monster High, I mean seriously, have you seen Holt Hyde? Which Monster High hottie would be your perfect after-life partner? Frankie has been working on a cool chart in Mr. Mummy's clawculus class to help you find out.
Want some answers?
Better do the monster math!

Read the chart, choosing a ➕ for every square that sounds like you and a ➖ sign for every statement that's soooo not your style. Follow the arrows to find out which gorgeous ghoul the formula will lead you to!

I'm a sucker for the monster-next-door look

My fave color is teal, fur-real!

I'm into flashy dressers!

On a dead-cool dinner date I always opt for Greek food

I want a sporty type who can give me a run for my money

I'd love to see in midnight, making spooky shapes on the dance floor

CLAWD WOLF™

You'd love to howl at the Moon with athletic Clawd by your side. In your eyes, he's the pack leader, even though he sheds ... a lot. Too bad he's taken! Draculaura's a lucky girl!

HOLT HYDE™

You like it hot, and they certainly don't get much toastier than Holt Hyde! The after-life is never dull when this monster's around. Holt's smokin' style and fiery personality is enough to keep any ghoulfriend on her toes.

Eeek! It's Exam Time

Oh My Ghoul, it's SAT time at Monster High! The students are all studying hard for the dreaded annual Scary Aptitude Test—a nightmare exam that is always 100% gruelling and fur-raising.

Uh-oh! It's your turn to take the test! This SAT paper is based on the school itself. Will you make the gruesome grade or score a voltagious fail? Grab a pen and get scribbling.

1. What form do the lockers take at Monster High?

....

2. Which pupil believes his "humanness" sets him apart from the rest of the student body at Monster High?

....

3. If the campus is the area of the school above ground, what is the area of the school below ground called?

....

4. Complete the phrase "Pit of _ _ _ _ _ _", meaning a menacing area of the school avoided by students at all costs.

....

5. Draculaura is one of the oldest students currently registered at Monster High. What is her age?

....

6. Which ghoul at Monster High is a vegetarian?

....

7. Besides his talent for casketball, Deuce Gorgon is spookily gifted at which other subject on the scare-iculum?

....

8. Which unique capability makes Lagoona Blue an ideal captain for the Monster High swim team, as well as giving her an advantage against other students?

....

9. Which helpful service does Ghoulia Yelps wish her pet owl would perform for her?

....

10. If a gargoyle bulldog called Rockseena™ was running amok in the study howl, which monster would you return it to?

....

11. When would it be a bad idea to challenge a werewolf such as Clawdeen to an athletic challenge—especially in track?

....

12. KBLOOD 105 is very popular among the students. What is it?

....

13. Who has a social-networking alter-ego called Ghostly Gossip?

....

14. Why does Monster High run special evening classes?

....

15. Which coastal location is favored by Monster High students during Spring Break and other holidays?

....

16. Which aquatic monster has a crush on Gil?

....

17. Which exchange student is it good to sit next to on a boiling hot day?

....

18. Which clever Monster High student would you call on if you needed to hack a computer?

....

19. What is said to happen at Monster High every Friday the 13th?

....

20. Which Monster High student is scared of the dark?

....

Got your paper in?

Now check your answers on page 68 and turn back to see how you did.

1-6 POINTS

Ouch! Shuffle on down to the catacombs and join Mr. Where's extra classes for failing students. You'd better get down there quick, even if you are a zombie! Get any more results like this and your rents are sure to under-ground you for the rest of the year.

7-15 POINTS

OK, so it's not a spooktacular score, but it's not a fail either! Try creeping up to Ghoulia Yelps or Clawd Wolf in the study howl. Let Ghoulia show you some dusty old works by a mad professor or ask Clawd about the latest casketball scores and you'll have a new study partner before you can say "dead and buried".

16-20 POINTS

You go, ghoul! Fangtastic first effort on the SAT, you've really got to grips with the undead! With a score like this you're sure to ace the rest of the papers. Just wait for the next Parent-Creature Conference. Your folks are going to be dead proud!

Fix Fright Tube

When they're not chowing down in the creepateria or doing extra fearleading practice, the students love to spend their lunch hour checking out FrightTube. Frankie's just logged on to see if any scarily cool clips have been posted.

Ulch! The movies aren't loading properly today. Can you help? Pick the clip you'd most like to see from the selections on the right, then draw them onto the screens.

www.frighttube.com

Fright Tube | Monster High 🔍

Create Account | Sign In

Monster High ••••••••••••••••••••••••••••

DE NILE GOES WILD!
Check out the moment when Cleo found out that I, Nefera, had been drafted in to fix her horrific Fear Squad™.
Posted by Nefera de Nile

RAMPAGING NIGHTMARE
Headmistress Bloodgood's trusty steed gets spooked by Perseus™, Deuce's rat.
Posted by Clawd Wolf

GHOULS' NIGHT IN
Frankie, Ula D and Clawdeen in da House! Check out what we got up to at our Saturday night creepover in Frankie's "Fab".
Posted by Draculaura

Monster High [search field]

Monster High ....

SCARY CUTE KITTY

My scary cute kitty Crescent on the prowl. Watch out Perseus—there's a new cat in town!
Posted by Clawdeen Wolf

MUSIC MADNESS

Jammin' with my ghoul Operetta. I love getting on the decks while she plays that guitar. No singing though! Don't want to lose my mind….
Posted by Holt Hyde

GHOULIA RULES
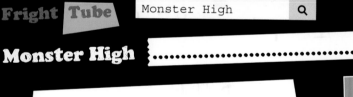
Couldn't help sharing Ghoulia's ghastly achievements! This is my ghoul at the Mad Science Fair—she took first prize for her invention for trimming unwanted fur. Werewolves take note, you're going to want one of these!
Posted by Mrs Yelps

Monster High [search field]

Monster High ....

FUR FLIES IN THE WOLF PACK

Things always get a little kerazy at our den on a full moon. Here's what happened last month when Clawdeen discovered Howleen had been in her wardrobe without asking … again.
Posted by Clawnor Wolf™

CASKETBALL CHAOS

Clawd and Deuce go for the casket at the same time and Deuce's glasses slip off. Ouch! Let's just say things get rocky for Clawd!
Posted by Jackson Jekyll

LAGOONA'S PURSE

Here's what went down when Holt Hyde accidentally dropped his headphones into Lagoona's purse.
Posted by Cleo de Nile

Dear Oracle...

Check out the latest issue of *Teen Scream* Magazine. Can you guess which Monster High student has anonymously written in for advice from the all-knowing Oracle? Scrawl the right sign-off underneath each letter, then check your answers on page 68.

1.

Dear Oracle,

It very difficult is to be having to write in to a magazine but when you are exchange student you do not having any family to talk to—and anyway because of thinness of air in mountains, my family do not like to do the talking too much anyhow. So I am writing to you the Oracle for hoping that you can think how I can make bigger my friendships in new school. So far, I have only two ghouls who are giving me the time of night. I think because sometimes what I am having in my heart and what is coming from my lips are not the same thing and they think I am rude. What must I do to make better understand me, these people?

With the sincerest of my regards to you,

Abby

2.

Dear Oracle,

Can you die from love if you are already undead? I think I might be in danger of this happening to me! There is a totes ughsome guy at school who almost restarts my heart every time I see him. We are kind of dating, but I am friends with one of his family members and it's a little awkward at times. Should I cool it so my GFF feels happier, even though being without him feels like being stuck outside on a sunny day?

Yours achingly,

Draculaura

3.

DEAR ORACLE,
I TOTALLY HOPE THAT YOU CAN HELP ME BECAUSE I AM LIKE, ON THE VERGE OF DOING SOMETHING REVOLTAGE! THERE'S THIS CERTAIN SOMEONE WHO IS TOTALLY RUINING MY LIFE. THE GHOUL IN QUESTION DOES EVERYTHING IN HER POWER TO MAKE ME FEEL SMALL AND TO MESS THINGS UP FOR ME. I JUST DISCOVERED THAT SHE'S BEEN KEEPING A MAJOR SECRET FROM MY DAD WHO (FALSELY) THINKS SHE'S THE ASP'S ELBOW! SHOULD I BLOW HER COVER AND TELL HIM SHE'S LOST HER JOB?

LATERS,

Cleo de Nile

4.

Dear Oracle,
Me and another guy are trapped in the most bizarre love triangle ever! We both like the same ghoul. I hardly ever see him around school—I think he must skip class a lot (how lame?) and I don't like the sound of him at all. But I've been having these blackouts and the other day, the ghoul of my night-mares brings me around and tells me that me and this other guy—we're like the same person. I don't know what to think, it sounds crazy, but she's a pretty switched-on, high-voltage ghoul. After this, she gave me the cold shoulder. What's my next move?

From,

Jackson Jekyll

41

Lunchtime Horrorscopes

The latest issue of *Teen Scream* is out and the horrorscopes make fangscinating reading! Astro-newbie Frankie is totally hooked. Want to know what your year has in store? Find your sign and read on.....

Ascaryius
January 20 – February 18
You've been feeling woefully gloomy all month long, but resist the urge to take this ghastly mood out on your ghoulfriends. By the summer you'll be floating on air, just like a ghost on Friday the 13th.

Die-ces
February 19 – March 20
You're all set to meet the monster of your nightmares! Stay dead calm and be your ugh-mazing, scary-cool self. Remember—if the guy or ghoul in question is a zombie, you'll need to be r-e-a-l-l-y patient.

Scaries
March 21 – April 19
Your ghoulfriends know you best, so if you want advice ask your GFF. Reaching your ghastly goals is entirely possible this year—work hard and you're sure to be scarily productive.

Clawrus
April 20 – May 20
A ghoul you know is on a mission to rattle your chains, making you want to run screaming back to your tomb just to get out of their way. Don't freak, dig your claws in and stay put. You're totally clawsome!

Gemacabre
May 21 – June 20
Don't be afraid of making an utter ghoul of yourself! Continue your bold new attitude, especially when it comes to trying out new things. Want to try casketball? Give it a shot. Thinking about joining Fear Squad? Why not! The crypt's the limit!

Cancertifiable
June 21 – July 22
Some ghostly gossip you thought was totally in the coffin has made its way to the ears of a rival. Don't let the tittle-tattle phase you, just go about your ghastly business. How about a spontaneous trip to the maul for some retail therapy?

Howl-eo
July 23 – August 22
A close relationship needs some TLC (tender loving claws) on Wednesday. Prioritize this or there could be a monster break-up on the cards. Beware of divulging your darkest secrets to a stranger with evil intentions.

Virghostly
August 23 – September 22
Embrace your imperfections this week. You've been feeling a little bleak so spend a few minutes checking out your killer self in the mirror—unless you're a vampire, in which case ask a friend to remind you how totally ughsome you are.

Libraaaaagh!
September 23 – October 22
You love sleeping by day so you can get up to all sorts of spooky shenanigans by night. Make sure you get that clawculus assignment done so you can really let your fur down and howl at the Moon.

Scorpion
October 23 – November 21
It's a case of opposites don't attract at school right now and the fur will fly, but put your claws away and try to communicate. The new year brings the opportunity to clear the air. You'll feel better for it!

Sagit-hairy-us
November 22 – December 21
Your weird and wacky antics are a puff of stale air round Monster High. People will try to put you back in your coffin, but don't listen to their screeches. You are freaky and fabulous.

Creepicorn
December 22 – January 19
You may wish you could come apart at the seams and be in two places at once, but don't worry, you'll cope. Once you get your head down and your fangs into something, you can't help but succeed.

42

Pet Pals

Oh no! Ghoulia has lumbered into Deuce en route to lunch and knocked his sunglasses flying. Now he's on his way back to his locker to get a spare pair of shades, trying to look at the floor so none of his fellow students get turned to stone.

Although Deuce's classmates are cool, his gaze couldn't help falling on several of their critters. Check out their solidified shapes! Can you scribble the right name, species and owner next to each one?

1.

NAME: ....

SPECIES: Rat ....

OWNER: Dracuhra

2.

NAME: ....

SPECIES: Dog ....

OWNER: Frankie

3.

NAME: ....

SPECIES: ....

OWNER: ....

4.

NAME: ....

SPECIES: ....

OWNER: ....

5.

6.

NAME: ....

SPECIES: ....

OWNER: ....

NAME: ....

SPECIES: ....

OWNER: ....

NAME: ....

SPECIES: ....

OWNER: ....

43

Once Upon A Slime ...

Lou Zarr loves to give homework—it makes him feel as if he's part of the Monster High faculty, instead of a mere substitute creature. Eager Ula D can't wait to get started on his latest creative writing assignment! The students have been asked to imagine a scary story. How will yours begin?

Creepy Characters

Who will star in your terrifying tale? Your ghoulfriends and frenemies at Monster High, one of the beasties below or a brand-new monster of your own?

* Scarlett the Skeleton's daughter
* Nestor and Vanda the Loch Ness Monster's twin children
* Esme the Seawitch's daughter
* Orlando, nephew of the Ogre

Woeful Words

Use a smattering of these adjectives to add an awful atmosphere to your story.

* Hideous
* Horrific
* Terrible
* Gruesome
* Shocking
* Forbidding
* Scary
* Creepy
* Hair-raising
* Eerie
* Spinechilling

Spooky Spots

Will the story unfold at Monster High, or in one of these grim locations?

* The Coffin Bean (coffee shop)
* The Maul
* Gloom Beach
* Skull Shores
* The Bleak Bowl (bowling alley)
* Smogsnorts Vampyr Academy

Ghoulish Goings On

The first line is always the toughest. You could start with one of these....

* Urrrgh, gurrrr! Three zombies lurched across the sand at Gloom Beach....
* It was just another day in this monster's unlife....
* The lights went up and a thousand howls filled the air as Justin Biter walked on stage....
* The ghouls had never known a night like this....

44

Once upon a slime ...

Scary Cool Case

The ghouls at Monster High know that they're all unique, so they're big into personalizing school stuff to make it their own! Check out Cleo de Nile's clever guide for creating a scarily cool pencil case that's truly special.

YOU WILL NEED:
- TRACING PAPER
- PENCIL
- SCISSORS
- SEWING PINS
- A PLAIN CANVAS OR CLOTH PENCIL CASE IN THE COLOR OF YOUR CHOICE
- FABRIC PENS IN BLACK, PINK AND WHITE (PLUS EXTRA COLORS TO DECORATE)
- WHITE GLUE
- GOLD GLITTER OR TINY GOLD BEADS

1. TAKE YOUR SHEET OF TRACING PAPER AND CAREFULLY TRACE AROUND THE MONSTER HIGH SKULL EMBLEM.

2. CUT THE SKULL SHAPE OUT AND PIN IT TO THE FABRIC OF THE PENCIL CASE. POSITION IT WHEREVER YOU'D LIKE IT TO GO.

3. NOW DRAW CAREFULLY AROUND THE OUTLINE WITH YOUR PENCIL OR PEN.

4. UNPIN THE TEMPLATE AND GO OVER THE OUTLINE WITH A BLACK FABRIC PEN. FILL IN THE EYES AND NOSE AND THE OUTLINE OF THE BOW. USE A WHITE PEN TO FILL IN THE SKULL AND A PINK ONE TO COLOR THE BOW.

5. DRAW YOUR FIRST INITIAL ONTO THE CASE IN WHITE GLUE.

6. SPRINKLE THE GLITTER OR THE BEADS ONTO THE GLUE AREA BEFORE IT DRIES. LEAVE IT FOR A FEW MOMENTS THEN SHAKE OFF THE EXCESS. REPEAT WITH YOUR OTHER INITIAL OR INITIALS.

7. WHEN YOUR CASE IS DRY YOU CAN REPRODUCE THE DESIGN ON THE OTHER SIDE OR CREATE YOUR OWN UNIQUE STAMP USING THE FABRIC PENS. TOTALLY GOLDEN!

DON'T BE UNCOOL! ASK AN ADULT BEFORE USING SCISSORS AND SEWING MATERIALS.

Skull Shore Shenanigans

Lagoona Blue has agreed to meet Gilington Webber™ at Skull Shores in Polynesia, but it's a long ocean journey. Gil, the son of a river monster, is feeling totes exhausted. The confused creature has got himself lost in a spooky maze of caves outside of the harbor.

Can you help Lagoona find him?

Start

Finish

Doom At GLOOM BEACH
Part 2

Cleo's Fear Squad was spending more time dusting than dancing....

Those Smugsnorts Vampyr snobs will do anything to win!

None of the other girls are doing chores like us.

Luckily Cleo and Ghoulia had worked out an ultra-hot routine....

That's right Ghoulia, it's been scientifically designed to win.

Uugh!

We start with a double jive handwheel....

Frankie began to film the routine on her iCoffin to show her parents. Unfortunately, the werecats were on the prowl....

I was just finishing my video letter to my folks.

Instead the creep showed the vid to the opposition....

Wanna watch the Monster High routine again? Thought so!

I can mail it for you!

Later, Frankie had a visitor....

Try Fearleading!

Want to give Cleo de Nile and the gang a run for their money at the Monster Mashionals? Round up your most creeperific ghoulfriends and set up a fearsome new fearleading squad!

SCARY STYLE

Fearleading ghouls need to look the part! Raid your claw-set for killer clothes that will allow you to move while looking dead cool. Don't worry if you can't lay your paws on a set of fearleading uniforms—being a monster is all about embracing your uniqueness. Simply pick a theme color for the squad, then add your own twist with accessories that are totally "you".

MONSTER MAKE-UP

For that extra Monster High touch use face paints to add fangs, a ghoulish pallor or a Draculaura inspired heart-shaped beauty mark.

PAWFECT POM POMS

No fearleading squad is complete without pom poms! The Monster High ghouls shake black, pink or a combination of the two, but you can pick any shade to complement your fiercely fabulous look.

MAD MOVES

These mad moves are so this century, they are guaranteed to send shivers up the spines of any rival! Work some of these into your fearleading routines.

Cleo's Kick

This move is Cleo's trademark. Stand side by side and place one arm on your GFF's shoulder. Kick the opposite leg high in the air. If you're really flexible you could try kicking to the side and holding your leg up near your ear, by the ankle. Other squad members add drama by kneeling, putting their palms together above their head and moving their head side to side like an Egyptian.

Roarsome Roll

Kneel in a row, then do synchronized forward and backward rolls. When you find your feet, jump up and howl at the Moon!

Clawdeen's Claws

Make claws with your hands then "pounce" on imaginary prey.

Stein's Stalk Shimmy

Stalk to the left and then to the right for four paces. Next shimmy your shoulders back and forth, while shaking your pom poms.

The Ghoulia Lurch

Put your arms forward like a zombie and lurch forward for four steps and back for four. Now move to the right for four and to the left for four.

Terrifying Tunes

Fearleading routines need truly creeperific backing music! Why not set your routine to the fangtastic Monster High theme?

Walking down a darkened hallway
Everybody turns to look at you
It's not because you're different
It's just because you're so scary cool

A sinister style, mystery with a smile
You're drop dead gorgeous,
drop dead gorgeous
This school gives me the creeps,
but when I'm with my peeps
You can't ignore us
This is where the ghoul kids rule!

Monster, Monster High
Monster High
Monster, Monster High
Come on, don't be shy
Monster High
The party never dies

Monster, Monster High
Monster High
Monster, Monster High
Freaky chic, and fly
Monster High
Where student bodies lie

Hey, Frankie's got me fallin' apart
Oh, Draculaura's stealin' my heart
Clawdeen Wolf, you make me howl
at the Moon
Lagoona, you're the finest fish
in this lagoon
Cleo de Nile, you so beguile
Even though you act so vile (uh huh)
And Deuce has stone-cold style
These are my boos, my skeleton crew
A little strange, but so are you
Don't you wanna be a monster, too?

57

UGHH-MAZING SNEAKERS

When she's not in class, "wolf in chic clothing" Clawdeen can either be found on the soccer field or sketching designs at Fashion Entrepreneur Club. When shooting goals Clawdeen wears specially customized peep-toe, wedge trainers. Here, she shows you how to personalize your own pumps with a fangtastic Monster High twist. You'll truly stand out from the crowd!

ALWAYS ASK AN ADULT BEFORE CUSTOMIZING CLOTHES—YOU DON'T WANT TO BE UNDER-GROUNDED!

YOU WILL NEED:
• A pair of plain white canvas sneakers or hi-tops
• Fabric glue
• Paintbrush
• Sequins and beads in your favorite colors
• Textile or fabric marker pens in vibrant colors
• Colored laces

1 Wipe the sneakers to make sure they are clean. Allow them to dry and remove the laces.

2 To add some bling, paint a small area of the toe with fabric glue and carefully cover it with sequins.

3 Repeat the process until the whole toe-cap is covered. Don't try glueing the whole toe at one time or you'll end up rushing to finish the job before the glue dries.

4 Now it's time to personalize your pumps with your fabric pens. You could add your own graffiti style tags, freestyle draw a Monster High character or take inspiration from the fangtastic icons below.

5 When your sneakers look really colorful, finish the job with new laces in a vibrant and contrasting shade.

FOR AN EXTRA-SPECIAL TOUCH, WHY NOT THREAD SPARKLY BEADS ONTO YOUR LACES?

Shoes by ... you!
What will your ughh-mazing sneakers look like?

Hold The Front Page

Draculaura is a budding photographer, while Spectra is a journalist in training. The pair spend their time after school at the Monster High Newspaper Club honing their journalistic skills. They've almost finished working on the latest issue of the *Monster High Mail* but the print deadline is looming and a power outage means the office has been plunged into darkness. Can you help them by finishing the news stories and headlines, and captioning the photos?

The Monster High Mail

FEAR SQUAD SET FOR MASHIONALS

The Monster High fearleading squad led by Cleo de Nile triumphed last week at the Gloom Beach Fearleading Championship.

The Monster High Mail

Holt Hyde has confirmed that he will be DJ-ing at the forthcoming Dawn Of The Dead Dance. "I've been scratching and mixing it up, practicing my set down in the catacombs for months now," said the hot-headed student. "No-one drops dead-cool tunes like the Hyde!"
Headmistress Bloodgood added, "We are delighted that Holt has signed on for the gig. It will be the highlight of the students' social calendar! However we do hope that there will not be a repeat of last year's dance off, which turned ugly when a student's gown was ripped by another monster's careless claws."
Tickets for the dance can be purchased from Mr. Where in the Drama Department.

Frightday The 13th

Cleo and the ghouls were horrified to discover that Toralei was the new editor of The Fearbook....

... and mortalfied when she photo'd them getting soaked by the werecat sisters.

Why didn't I know Toralei was running the Fearbook?

Out of the loop? I AM the loop!

You're probably just out of the loop because fearleading took up so much time.

Didn't you know, Cleo? Everyone's wearing boas.

Worried Cleo tried using her father's cursed idols....

This can't be happening!

Mighty totem, fierce and mean, make me queen of the social scene.

... but this just brought about a plague of frogs!

I'll never regain my position atop the school social pyramid!

Me and my ghouls are all over it! We're not afraid of anything.

If anyone stayed overnight on Friday the 13th, they'd be the talk of the school for sure!

"You want to spend the night on Friday the 13th? You face a night of unknowable horrors ... no one's ever made it the whole night."

With a "Nightmare, tally-ho!", the principal fled the building.

The ghouls arrived for their creepover....

They say that once the sun sets a creature lurks about the halls, prowling for victims.

But....

Ladies it's clearly just a rumor....

YOWWWLLLL!!

YOWWWLLLL!!

Sssshhhh!

The beast's howls were just unhappy cries. Friday the 13th was its birthday! The ghouls knew just what to do.

They threw him a monster makeover birthday party!

The next morning....

Best. Night. Ever.

Toralei couldn't wait to hear all the gory deets.

The ghouls introduced their new friend....

But how? ... Aaargh!

THE END

FEARBOOK

Sneaky Toralei has got her hands on the first draft of this year's Fearbook. Can you complete the captions before the cruel kitty has a chance to get her claws and fangs into everyone? You'll need to decide what each student is most likely to do or achieve in the future.

DRACULAURA

Most likely to ...

marry her Monster High sweetheart (in black of course).

FRANKIE STEIN

Most likely to ...

spark up a conversation!

ABBEY BOMINABLE

Most likely to ...

say mean stuff

LAGOONA BLUE

Most likely to ...

Swim

SPECTRA VONDERGEIST

Most likely to ...

Say BOO!

CLEO DE NILE

Most likely to ...

Be popular

GHOULIA YELPS

Most likely to ...

Stare at her computer

OPERETTA

Most likely to ...

Rock out with her Guitar

CLAWDEEN WOLF

Most likely to ...

Get yelled at from her sister

Sleepover Secrets

There are ten mysterious differences between these photos. Can you circle them all?

Frankie's hosting a creepover in her basement lab (or as she calls it, the Fab!). All her ghoulfriends have floated by for a night of monster makeovers, scary human movies, furbulous pampering, and ghostly gossip.

Something is spookily wrong in both photos. Can you spot what it is? .... yes ....

At The Maul

Frankie and Ula D have just been to the Maul. Besides picking out cool new outfits for school, the GFFs have bought an electrifying total of nine purses between them. Well, with Homecarnage just around the corner a ghoul needs to keep her accessory options open!

Use colored pencils to draw in the rest of this shopping Sudoku grid. Make sure that each bag features only once in each row, column and small square.

Answers

IN THE STUDY HOWL WITH ... GHOULIA YELPS
Ghoulia's History Homework
1. Yeti
2. c. Transylvania
3. Pyramids
4. a. Silver
5. False. She turned her hair into snakes
6. Scotland

Pages 20–21
IN THE STUDY HOWL WITH ... SPECTRA VONDERGEIST
Spectra's Slimetable
MONDAY
Lesson 1: HOME ICK – Ms. Kindergrubber
Lesson 2: BITEOLOGY – Mr. Hackington
Lesson 3: DEAD LANGUAGES – Mr. Rotter
Lesson 4: PHYSICAL DEADUCATION – Coach Igor
TUESDAY
Lesson 1: DEAD LANGUAGES – Mr. Rotter
Lesson 2: DRAMA – Mr. Where
Lesson 3: CLAWCULUS – Mr. Mummy
Lesson 4: GE-OGRE-PHY – Mr. Lou Zarr
WEDNESDAY
Lesson 1: DRAGONOMETRY – Mr. Mummy
Lesson 2: DRAGONOMETRY – Mr. Mummy
Lesson 3: BITEOLOGY – Mr. Hackington
THURSDAY
Lesson 1: DRAMA – Mr. Where
Lesson 3: CLAWCULUS – Mr. Mummy
Lesson 4: DEAD LANGUAGES – Mr. Rotter
FRIDAY
Lesson 1: PHYSICAL DEADUCATION – Coach Igor
Lesson 2: DEAD LANGUAGES – Mr. Rotter
Lesson 4: FIZZ-ICKS – Mr. Hackington

Pages 22–23
IN THE STUDY HOWL WITH ... ABBEY BOMINABLE
"Your eyebrows, they are like mountains." – Clawdeen Wolf
"People around here talk too much about too little,
sometimes is better to just close the mouth." – Frankie Stein
"You are short – like baby Yak." – Draculaura
"This outfit, I think you try much too hard." – Cleo De Nile

Pages 30–31
Cleo and Deuce's Dead-Secret Code
Hi Deuce,
I've told Ghoulia we'll take her to the Coffin Bean after
school today and that you're paying. Oh and by the way,
I'm throwing a party on Saturday night. Be there and
look fangtastic!
Cleo

Hey Cleo,
Do I really have to pay … again? You know I love to treat
you, but I'm trying to save up. And before you totally like,
lose your bandages, it's for a surprise for you. I'll give it to
you at your party.
Deuce

Page 32–33
GRIM GRID

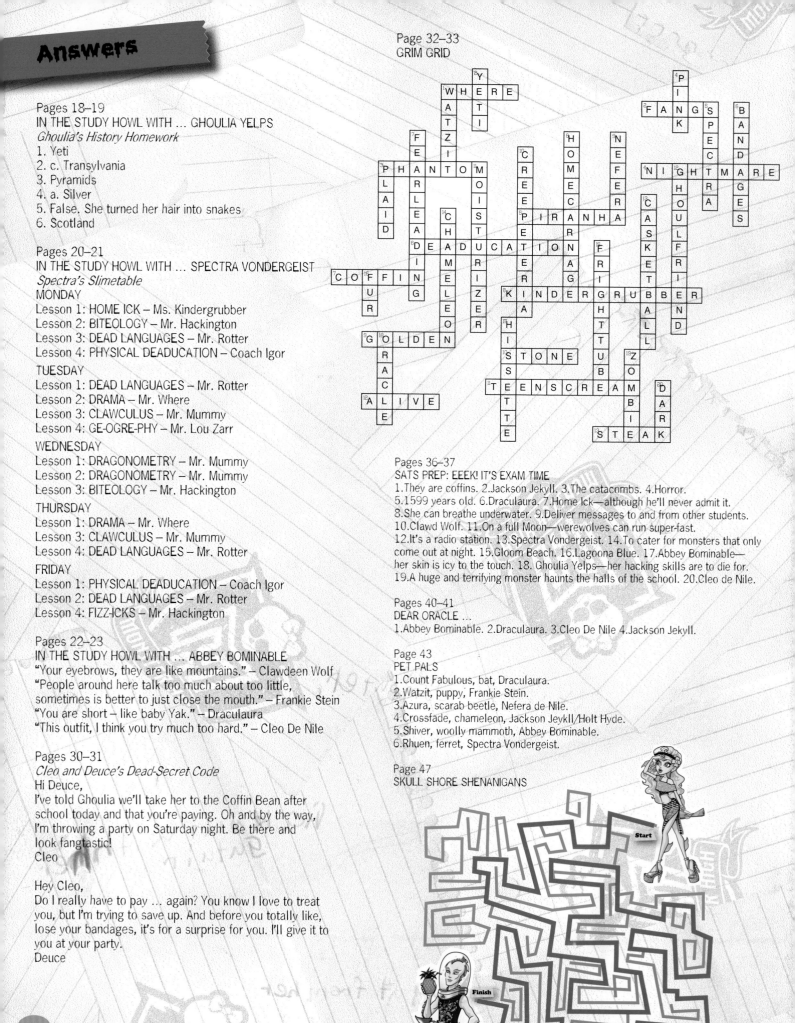

Pages 36–37
SATS PREP: EEEK! IT'S EXAM TIME
1. They are coffins. 2. Jackson Jekyll. 3. The catacombs. 4. Horror.
5. 1599 years old. 6. Draculaura. 7. Home Ick—although he'll never admit it.
8. She can breathe underwater. 9. Deliver messages to and from other students.
10. Clawd Wolf. 11. On a full Moon—werewolves can run super-fast.
12. It's a radio station. 13. Spectra Vondergeist. 14. To cater for monsters that only
come out at night. 15. Gloom Beach. 16. Lagoona Blue. 17. Abbey Bominable—
her skin is icy to the touch. 18. Ghoulia Yelps—her hacking skills are to die for.
19. A huge and terrifying monster haunts the halls of the school. 20. Cleo de Nile.

Pages 40–41
DEAR ORACLE …
1. Abbey Bominable. 2. Draculaura. 3. Cleo De Nile 4. Jackson Jekyll.

Page 43
PET PALS
1. Count Fabulous, bat, Draculaura.
2. Watzit, puppy, Frankie Stein.
3. Azura, scarab beetle, Nefera de Nile.
4. Crossfade, chameleon, Jackson Jeykll/Holt Hyde.
5. Shiver, woolly mammoth, Abbey Bominable.
6. Rhuen, ferret, Spectra Vondergeist.

Page 47
SKULL SHORE SHENANIGANS

Page 66
SLEEPOVER SECRETS
What is wrong with both photos? Draculaura's face has appeared in Cleo's mirror. Vampires can never see their reflections!

Page 67
AT THE MAUL

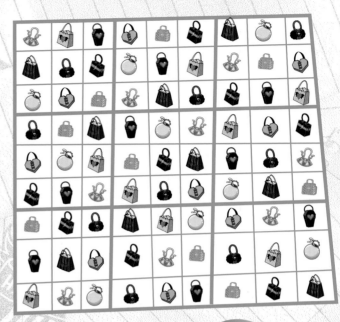

GHOULISH BOOKS

FEARBOOK
Over CREE STI

CLAWSOME Activities
WITH 11 FANGTASTIC STICKERS!
COOL GHOUL GAMES, creeperific quizzes, and SCARY-CUTE THINGS TO MAKE!

MONSTER PARTY
YOUR TOTALLY CLAWSOME
Ghoulish decorations ghoulish games and fangtastic food!

COMING SOON!

FANG-TASTIC!!

Available from all good booksellers and online